Santabear Books is an exclusive imprint of Dayton Hudson Department Store Company and
B. Dalton Bookseller, Minneapolis, Minnesota.

Produced for Santabear Books by dilithium Press, a division of OBC, Inc.

ISBN 0-8081-6301-9

SANTABEAR'S FIRST CHRISTMAS

Illustrations by Howard B. Lewis

Story by Barbara Read

Adapted by Thomas Roberts from *Santabear's First Christmas*,
produced and directed by Mark Sottnick

SANTABEAR BOOKS

Way, way up in the cold, cold north lives a very special snowy white bear. His name is Santabear. Oh, that wasn't always his name. He earned it on his very first Christmas. This is how it happened.

One day, before the coldest part of winter had arrived, the little snow bear and his family were fishing on the ice beside the enormous ocean.

Suddenly, a terrible, thundering sound rumbled through the air. All around the little bear, the ice began to crack. "Mother! Father! Help me!" he cried. But the ice broke apart with a frightening roar and he began to float away into the ocean.

His father and mother watched helplessly as their precious little cub sailed off alone on the cold and stormy sea.

The little bear scraped at the slippery ice and held on as tightly as he could. Huge waves splashed over him. The fish he had caught was washed back into the ocean.

The little snow bear was alone, all alone.

Suddenly, a mighty gust of wind snatched him up, and he spun and tumbled and whirled through the air.

Then, the little bear landed—*plop!* He looked up and saw that he was surrounded by hundreds of tall brown arms. He was frightened. He was afraid that the arms would reach down and pluck him up and carry him off.

The little snow bear trembled and closed his eyes and thought about his mother and father. He curled into a white furry ball. Even with his eyes shut tight, big tears rolled down his fuzzy cheeks.

Before long, he heard footsteps coming closer and closer. They stopped. The little bear sprang up and started to run off. But a gentle, friendly voice called to him:

"Don't run away." He stopped and turned to see a little girl. "Don't be afraid, little bear." And suddenly he wasn't afraid anymore. "I want to be your friend," she said. "My name is Marie. What's yours?"

The little bear just stared at her, and then he smiled.

Marie took his hand and they walked off together. He told Marie how frightened he was of those gigantic brown arms. But she only laughed. "Those are trees, little bear. They won't hurt you at all. They help to keep us warm." And, for the first time since he was with his family, the little bear felt safe. "Why don't you come to my house for something to eat?" asked Marie.

He thought that was a fine idea.

Just ahead, in a clearing, was a cabin. "This is where I live," said Marie, opening the door. "Come in."

The cabin seemed so bright and warm that the little snow bear scurried right through the door.

Inside, he skidded to a stop and looked at a very strange creature across the room. It was orange and yellow and red all at the same time, and it crackled and crunched and popped in a most unusual way. The frightened little bear turned to run away.

"Don't be afraid," said Marie. "This is fire. It keeps us warm and lights our cabin and cooks our food. See? Our dinner is almost ready."

Sure enough, the food in the pot began to bubble and boil. It smelled delicious. The little bear's nose twitched, and he suddenly realized how awfully hungry he was.

Just then, the cabin door opened and in walked Marie's grandfather, a cheery old man with bright, crinkly eyes and a sunny smile.

"Welcome," said Grandfather. "Please sit down and eat with us."

The little bear sniffed the bowl of food and sighed. Then he scooped out some food with his paw.

"This is strange fish. But it is very tasty," he said politely, licking his paw. He had never tasted anything like this before.

"But it isn't fish at all!" laughed Marie. "It's porridge with honey and milk and berries and nuts on top."

The bear soon forgot how lonely he was and ate everything in sight.

After dinner, he yawned and rubbed his sleepy eyes with his furry paw. Grandfather picked him up and tucked him into a soft, warm, wonderful bed. The bear was so tired that he fell asleep right away.

As it grew to be winter, Marie taught the little bear how to make cookies, how to dance, and how to read. Most of all, though, he loved listening to Marie tell stories of circuses and sea voyages, of kings and castles, of pirates and princesses. And he would tell her stories of his life in the far, far north.

Together they explored the forest, meeting most of the animals who lived there. They met some brown bears. He and the brown cubs would chase each other around the towering trees and roll and play endlessly in the snow. And when the brown cubs would get all covered with snow, they reminded the little bear of his own brothers and sisters.

Every night he went to bed and dreamed of his family in the far, far north.

Later on, as the winter winds howled, they spent more and more time in the cozy cabin.

One night, Marie told the little snow bear about a very special day called Christmas.

"On the night before Christmas," she began, "eight flying reindeer pull a sleigh across the sky. The driver is a jolly, kindhearted fellow with a big tummy and a white beard and red cheeks. His name is Santa Claus and he delivers Christmas presents to every child in the world in just one night."

"Truly this is a wonderful world to live in," thought the bear. And he drifted off to sleep, dreaming of flying reindeer and this jolly old gentleman.

Christmas Eve dawned and Grandfather felt terribly sick. He had fallen into the icy river. By the time he reached the cabin, he had icicles hanging all over him, his fingers and toes felt frozen, and his whole body was shaking.

"What shall we do, little bear?" sobbed Marie. "The firewood is running out." The little snow bear thought hard, harder than ever. He decided he must go out in the forest and get some firewood himself.

The bear rushed out the door and down the path and plunged—
kerplop—into a snowdrift, right up to his chin!

"Help!" he cried. "Help! Get me out! I have to save Grandfather!"

A big brown animal with branches on his head appeared out of
the forest.

"My name is Moose," said the animal. The little bear explained
why he had to find firewood. "I'll help you. Grab my antlers and
pull yourself up onto my back."

He carried the bear up the
frozen stream to the beaver
lodge.

But the beavers had used
all their wood. To chew down
more trees would take them
a long, long time.

By now it was getting dark.
The bear was heartbroken.
He would not be able to save
Marie's grandfather. Tears
rolled down his cheek and
plopped onto Moose's back.

Just then the little snow bear heard bells jingling above his head. He looked up and saw a red sleigh, pulled by eight reindeer, flying through the sky. It swooped down and landed right in front of Moose and the bear. Out climbed someone who could only be Santa Claus!

"Ho! Ho! Ho!" he laughed. "And who are you?" He looked at the little snow bear. "You must be new to this forest."

"I am. My real home is in the far, far north."

"So is mine," said Santa, with a twinkling smile. "And what would you like to have for Christmas? Nuts? Berries? A pot of honey? You can have anything you wish."

The little bear thought of his family and how very much he wanted to be with them.

But he said, "Firewood."

"Firewood?" said Santa with astonishment. "But bears don't build fires!"

Then the words began to tumble out of the little bear, about Marie and how sick her grandfather was. Santa nodded gravely and went over to the bulging pack on his sleigh.

Out of it he drew a small saw. He handed it to the bear. Then he took an axe from his toolbox and, with a few quick whacks, he cut some small trees.

"Now you saw the trees into logs," Santa said.

The bear tried the saw on the bark of a tree. It really cut! Soon he had a stack of logs almost as tall as he was.

Santa went back to his pack and pulled out a shiny red sled. Then Santa and the little bear quickly piled all the logs onto the sled.

When the sled was full, Santa jumped in his sleigh and led the way to Marie's cabin.

"Will we be in time?" worried the bear.

Inside the cabin, the fire was completely out and it was so cold that Marie could see her breath. She listened to her grandfather's troubled breathing and worried. Suddenly, she heard sleigh bells.

She ran to the window and saw eight beautiful reindeer pulling a magnificent sleigh carrying Santa Claus himself! Behind Santa was the little snow bear pulling a sled full of firewood!

Soon, a fire was blazing in the hearth and the smell of hot soup
filled the air. Marie's grandfather sat up and began to eat. His
cheeks turned rosy and his eyes began to sparkle.

Santa said, "You can thank this special fellow for your rescue."
The little bear smiled shyly.

Before long, Santa had to leave. After all, it was Christmas Eve
and he had a lot of presents to deliver.

He took the little snow bear outside. "I'm way behind in delivering my presents. Could you take these gifts to all the animals in the forest and to Marie and her grandfather for me?"

With that, Santa sprang into his sleigh, called out to his reindeer, waved to the little bear, and streaked off through the sky like a comet.

The bear set off with the packages. He delivered them high and low, up and down, in and out, and everywhere in between. And finally, when all the animals had their Christmas presents, the little bear fell into bed.

He was dreaming of his family when sleigh bells awakened him. He ran outside.

"Ho! Ho! Ho!" cried Santa when he saw the little snow bear. "You have done such a fine job that I want you to be my helper. From now on, your name will be Santabear. You shall deliver presents every Christmas Eve." Santa reached into his nearly empty pack.

"Here—your very own special hat and scarf!"

Santabear jumped up and down. He had never been so proud and so happy in all his life.

"And one more thing," Santa Claus said. "Your Christmas wish was for firewood. Isn't there anything you would like for yourself?"

Santabear gulped and said, "More than anything else, I would like to go home to my family."

"And so you will," replied Santa. "Your home is not very far from mine. I'll take you there myself. We can leave right away."

Santabear ran into the cabin and found Grandfather and Marie by the fire. Grandfather patted Santabear on his furry head and thanked him for saving his life.

Santabear turned to Marie. With tears in their eyes, they hugged each other. "Don't be sad, I'll see you next year," they both said.

Going back outside, Santabear wrapped his scarf around himself, pulled his hat down over his ears, and climbed into Santa's sleigh. He waved good-bye to Marie and her grandfather. And then they were off.

In minutes, they had left the forest behind and were flying over a dazzling white ice cap. Santabear could see something else below. It was his own family!

In no time at all, he was hugging and kissing his mother and his father and his brothers and sisters.

"We searched every day," said his father. "We never gave up hope."

"Oh, Mother, Father, I dreamed of you every night and…I've learned so much of people and trees and fire. And guess what? You must call me Santabear from now on."

They wanted to know how he got such a name.

"Well, that's a very long story," explained Santabear. "I'll have to start at the beginning."

And that's exactly what he did.

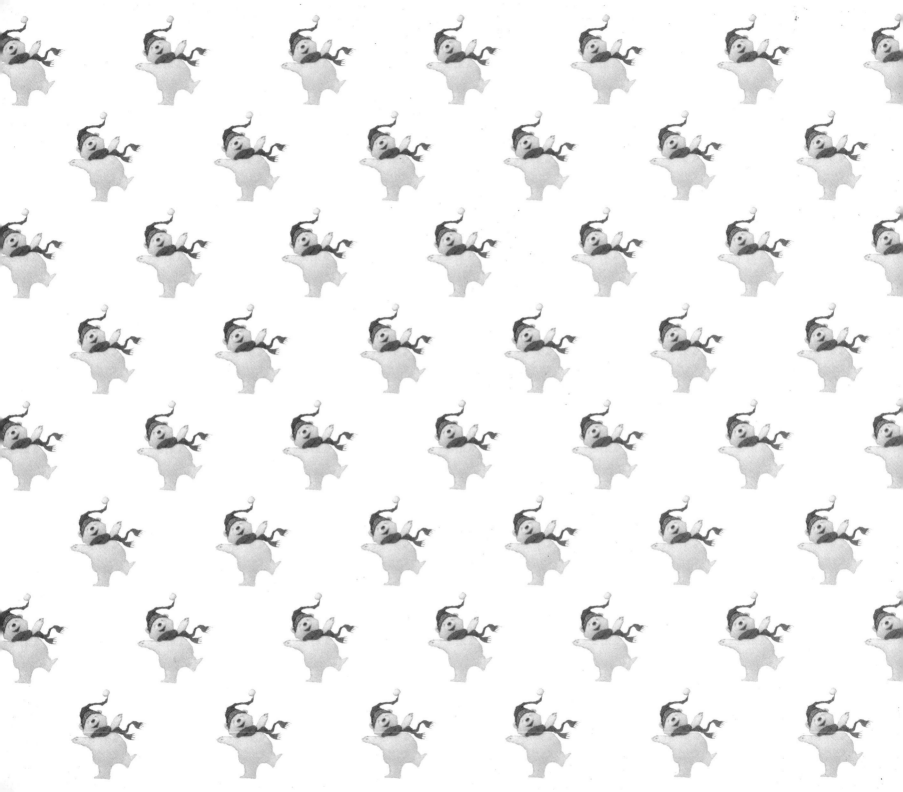